Lisa and the Lacemaker

Asperger Adventures

All Cats Have Asperger Syndrome
Kathy Hoopmann
ISBN 9 781 84310 481 0

Blue Bottle Mystery
An Asperger Adventure
Kathy Hoopmann
ISBN 978 1 85302 978 3

Of Mice and Aliens
An Asperger Adventure
Kathy Hoopmann
ISBN 978 1 85302 007 2

Lisa and the Lacemaker

An Asperger Adventure

Kathy Hoopmann

Jessica Kingsley Publishers
London and Philadelphia

First published in the United Kingdom in 2002
by Jessica Kingsley Publishers
116 Pentonville Road
London N1 9JB, UK
and
400 Market Street, Suite 400
Philadelphia, PA 19106, USA

www.jkp.com

Library of Congress Cataloging in Publication Data
A CIP catalog record for this book is available from the Library of Congress

British Library Cataloguing in Publication Data
A CIP catalogue record for this book is available from the British Library

ISBN 978 1 84310 071 3

For Becky

Contents

Chapter 1
The Party

"Come on, Lisa. We're late. Granny May's party started half an hour ago."

Lisa's Mum walked quickly down the garden path. Petunias grew in neat lines on each side. It all looked so formal, thought Lisa. Not a place for kids.

Lisa's footsteps slowed as she neared the door of the house. This was a place Lisa had never visited before and belonged to an uncle she could not remember. Through the windows there were people everywhere. Strangers to be polite to, who would ask her questions and try to hug her. She didn't want to go inside. Inside was noise and confusion.

Lisa pulled a blue satin scarf from her pocket. It had been her comfort rag for as long as she could remember and was patched and faded from wear. Stretching it under her chin, she rubbed each end against her ears. The softness was calming. And the brushing of the material blocked out all sound. She was herself again. But only for a moment.

"Lisa! Put that old thing away. You look silly when you do that! You don't want everyone to think you're strange, do you?" Without expecting an answer, Mum turned back and rang the doorbell. "And please… please behave yourself."

Lisa put away the scarf and stood tall, gathering the courage to last for a whole morning. Family get-togethers were horrible and to make things worse, the pretty dress Mum made her wear was dreadfully uncomfortable. She slid her finger between her neck and the lace frill and pulled. Too hard. She felt it tear but didn't mind. At least it now felt better.

Just as Mum reached again for the doorbell, an old man wearing a hat and braces opened the door. "Hello, Uncle Bert!" Mum said as she gave him a kiss. "Do you remember Lisa? She must have been about two last time you saw her."

The big man ruffled Lisa's hair and she cringed away. "Hello there. My, how you've grown," he said.

Lisa smelt smoke on his breath. "Cigarettes cause cancer," she said without looking at him. She heard his intake of breath, and her mother's nervous laugh. Mum will give me a talk about manners later, she thought. Telling the truth got her into trouble all the time. As Mum spoke to Uncle Bert, Lisa edged into the room and stood in a corner away from the crowd, searching for an escape route.

"Hi," a kind voice said.

Lisa did not raise her head. She stood still, hoping the person would go away.

"Who do you belong to?" the voice continued.

"I'm just me. I don't belong to anyone," Lisa said gruffly. She had to get away. Anywhere. Darting under the nearest table, she hid against the wall, shielded from view by the edges of the tablecloth. Panic grew in her chest, making it hard to breathe. Legs came up to the table and then went away. Legs in dresses. Legs in trousers. Some stood around for awhile. Some walked up and down. It didn't take long to realize she was sitting under the food table.

In the distance Mum was chatting to some stranger. So Lisa wasn't in trouble…yet. She crawled out, snatched a sandwich and ducked under the table again, then scrunched up her nose. Yuck. Ham. Actually there were very few things she did enjoy eating. Most foods tasted strange or yucky to her. They were either too lumpy or grainy or slippery or salty. But Paddy liked everything. Paddy was her much loved pet mouse and he went everywhere with her. Lisa coaxed Paddy out from her pocket and settled him on her knee. He nibbled happily on the sandwich.

"Lisa! What are you doing?" Mum lifted the tablecloth and glared at her daughter.

"Feeding Paddy," Lisa said.

"Get out from under there now! And why did you bring that mouse in here? I told you to behave!"

Lisa felt tears in her eyes. "I try to be good, Mum. I just don't know what you mean."

Mum stopped and thought. Maybe today was too much for her daughter. A strange place. Strange people. Her face softened. "I know you try, Lisa. And I know this is hard for you. But I want you to learn to get on with people. Why not talk to Granny May? At least you know her. Come on." Mum stretched out her hand. "I'll go with you."

Lisa slipped Paddy into her pocket and crawled out on her own. She didn't take her mother's hand. Holding hands hurt her fingers. She preferred not to be touched much.

They saw Granny May sitting on a lounge chair drinking tea from a delicate china cup with roses on it. "There," Mum said. "Now's a good chance to talk to your grandmother. Wish her happy birthday or something."

Lisa wandered reluctantly up to Granny May. "Happy birthday," she said quickly. "My mouse had seven babies last night. Paddy, he's the father mouse, ate one before we separated them. We found him munching on the carcass this morning."

Granny May spilt tea all over her shirt.

"Do you want to see him?" Lisa brought Paddy out of her pocket and put him on her grandmother's lap. Granny May screamed. Her teacup fell and smashed onto the floor. People came running from everywhere.

Lisa snatched up Paddy and fled out of the nearest door.

Chapter 2

Great Aunt Hannah

Outside were dozens of plants in pots and Lisa hid behind the largest one. Sniffing back tears, she stroked Paddy gently. Parties were horrible! Lisa had only ever had one party herself and it was a disaster. Kids came into *her* house and played with *her* toys and put things in all the wrong positions. They gave presents she didn't like and got upset when she told them so. She vowed never to have another party again.

"Lisa, are you all right?" Mum had followed Lisa outside.

Lisa nodded sullenly.

"Why did you put that mouse on your grandmother? You know she doesn't like them."

"I know, but I thought she'd like Paddy."

Mum sighed. Lisa always had a reason for what she did, but it could take an hour of long discussion to try to understand what that reason was. And sometimes the problem could be as simple as the way something was said to her. If Mum was to tell Lisa to look something up in the phone book, Lisa might sit up on a cupboard to do it. But today there wasn't enough time for a long talk with Lisa. Mum had to get back to the party.

"Well, this yard seems safe enough," she said. "Are you happy to stay out here a while?"

"Yes!"

"Keep out of mischief and I'll check on you from time to time. OK?"

"OK," Lisa agreed.

Now that there was no pressure to be with people, Lisa looked around curiously. What a boring yard. Lisa wanted to climb trees and get messy, but here everything was clipped and orderly. The grass was great though. Thick and healthy and green. Lisa lay on the grass enjoying the cool softness, watching the sky.

"What can you see in the clouds?" said a voice.

Lisa didn't move. Couldn't she be left alone?

"What about dragons? There are always dragons in clouds."

Lisa grinned. At least this person made sense. Raising her head, she saw an old lady in a wheelchair on the nearby path. She wore a puffy pink dress that spilled over the edge of the chair. There seemed to be more dress than woman.

"There's a dragon over there," Lisa said pointing to the right. "He's snarling."

"Blowing smoke," said the lady.

They watched the clouds in silence until the wind scattered their dreams.

"I'm Lisa Flint," Lisa said after a while. "Who are you?"

"I'm your Great Aunt Hannah," said the lady after a while, "but you can call me Aunt Hannah. Everyone else does."

"What makes you great?" Lisa asked.

"I'm your grandmother's sister, and therefore I am your Great Aunt and you are my Great Niece."

"Great!" Lisa laughed. She sat up and tugged at the lace of her dress. It was really irritating her neck. "Why are you in a wheelchair?"

"I'm old. My bones are worn out."

"Can you walk?"

"A bit."

"How do you go to the toilet?"

"The same as you." Aunt Hannah didn't mind all the questions, even though they were so personal.

"I've got a disability too," Lisa said.

"Really?"

"I've got Asperger Syndrome. Mum says it's a hidden disability because I look like other kids but really I'm different."

"I've never heard of Asperger Syndrome."

"It's on the autistic continuum," Lisa said in a matter of fact way.

Aunt Hannah chuckled. "Such big words from a little girl."

"I use big words all the time. Mum says that's because of my Asperger's."

"What exactly is this *Asperger's*?" Aunt Hannah asked, intrigued.

"The doctor said it's got something to do with my brain. Aspies, that's what we call ourselves, we don't really understand other people too well. Especially at parties."

Aunt Hannah laughed. "That's not so unusual. I've never understood other people either."

"Maybe you have Asperger's too?"

"I don't know, dear. Nobody has ever mentioned it to me."

Lisa was quiet for a moment, then said, "My Asperger brain helps me remember things, like poetry, but sometimes I wish I was the same as other kids. Then people wouldn't think I'm strange."

"Ahh, Lisa, never mind what others believe. As Robert Louis Stevenson once said, 'Make the most of the best and the least of the worst.'"

"I know him! He wrote *Treasure Island*."

"Clever girl," Aunt Hannah said.

"Do you like mice?" Lisa asked suddenly.

"I love mice."

Lisa got up and handed Paddy to the old lady. "He's beautiful," Aunt Hannah said as she gently stroked his fur.

Lisa felt good. She had found a friend.

Chapter 3

Lace

Lisa sat beside the wheelchair as Aunt Hannah played with Paddy. Curious, Lisa stroked the long skirt of the pink dress. It was made of soft velvet. Without thinking, she grabbed a handful of the material and rubbed her face in it. It was soft and almost furry and smelt of lavender. She stroked it against her ears, enjoying the whoosh of trapped air.

"It's lovely material, isn't it?" Aunt Hannah said, not at all bothered by Lisa's behaviour.

"It's heavenly."

"I'm always told that I should wear clothes more suitable for people my age, but I prefer pretty colours and beautiful fabrics and I don't care what others say."

"I agree," Lisa said. "But baggy clothes are my favourite. I hate *this* dress." She pulled at the collar again.

"What's wrong with it?" asked Aunt Hannah

"The lace is scratchy."

Aunt Hannah reached for Lisa's collar. Her hand was old and knobbly, but her grip was firm and before Lisa knew what was happening, Aunt Hannah ripped the lace off with one quick tug.

"Better?"

"Better," Lisa answered, pleased.

"Horrible stuff," Aunt Hannah said, fingering the prickly material. "It's only made to torture children."

"No it's not, Aunt Hannah. Lace is used on curtains and lots of things."

"Lace? This isn't lace. Lace is soft and beautiful. A poem from the heart twisted into thread."

Lisa wasn't sure how you twist a poem, but the words sounded lovely.

"I used to make lace, you know, before I got too old." Aunt Hannah held up gnarled fingers. "Learnt when I was your age. In fact, lace is part of me. Guess what my last name is."

"Lace?" Lisa said.

"Yes! Hannah Lace. That's me."

Lisa grinned. This old lady was OK. "Do you make lace on a loom, like weaving?" she asked.

"No, you use a pillow."

"A pillow?"

"A big fat hard one to pin the thread into position."

"That sounds fun."

"Actually, you remind me of lacemaking," said Aunt Hannah. "You're like a gimp."

"A gimp? What's that?" Lisa asked.

"Well, dear," Aunt Hannah paused. "It's very hard to explain a gimp without showing you how lace is actually made. Perhaps one day I could do that. But basically when you make lace you use a series of threads that come in pairs and you twist these together. But sometimes you can use a single thread to give an extra pattern to the lace. This thread, or "the gimp" as we call it, might be a different colour from the others. Or maybe a different texture. You're like that. A little girl who brings her own special pattern to the world."

Lisa grinned. "Lisa the gimp. That sounds good."

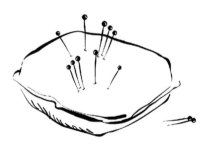

"Lisa!" Lisa's Mum called from a window. "Oh hello, Aunt Hannah. I hope my daughter hasn't been bothering you."

Aunt Hannah turned her chair towards the window. "Hello Mandy. Lisa's not bothering me at all. She's a delightful child."

"Good. Granny May's birthday cake has been cut. Do you want to come in and have some?"

"No," said Lisa and Aunt Hannah together. They laughed as if they shared a secret. As if they'd been friends for ever.

Lisa's Mum shrugged. At least Lisa was not getting into trouble out there. And Aunt Hannah had always been a loner. In fact, they made a good pair.

Chapter 4

Off to Ben's Place

The party was finally over. Lisa had managed to avoid all her relatives' goodbye kisses and now she flopped into the car seat and breathed deeply. They still faced a long drive home, which wasn't going to be much fun either. Three boring things in a row and it wasn't even lunchtime. The first was the long boring trip to Uncle Bert's, then the long boring party and now the long boring trip home. Mum put on her sunglasses and started the car.

"Mum," Lisa said, "Never take me to another party again, ever, pleeeease."

"But I thought you were having fun," Mum said, surprised. "You certainly got on well with Aunt Hannah."

"Yeah, she was nice. But she was the only good thing there. Can we visit her again?"

"I know she'd enjoy that. In fact she has recently moved into a nursing home not far from your school."

"Is she going to be nursed like a baby?"

Mum laughed as she drove out onto the road. "Not that kind of nursing. It's a place where people go when they can't care for themselves without help. Aunt Hannah will have her own little home, but there will be nurses and doctors checking on her every day. Anyway she asked if we could visit her tomorrow. I'm not sure if I should tell you this, but she said that she had something she wanted to give you."

"Really? How exciting. I wonder what it is?" Just then, Paddy poked his head out of her pocket and tested the air with twitchy-nosed sniffs. Lisa stroked him tenderly and he crawled onto her hand.

"Can I give Aunt Hannah a present too?" Lisa asked suddenly. "I want to give her a mouse. She thought Paddy was the cutest thing she'd seen in ages."

Mum smiled at the thought as she slowed to a stop at the traffic lights. "No darling. They don't allow mice in nursing homes."

"Why not? They'd be good company."

"They'd be a health risk."

"Mice?" Lisa shook her head. "Not if you keep the cage clean."

"Lisa, Aunt Hannah can't even walk. There's no way she could clean out a cage."

"She can walk a bit, but I'll clean the cage for her."

"No, sweetheart. It's simply not allowed."

"It's not fair."

"Maybe not, but rules are rules," Mum said as she concentrated on driving.

"What do you mean? Of course rules are rules."

"It means you have to obey rules even if you don't agree with them."

Using a long, drawn-out voice, Lisa said,

"I wouldn't stand by and see the rules broke — because right is right, and wrong is wrong, and a body ain't got no business doing wrong when he ain't ignorant and knows better."

Mum laughed. "Exactly!" she said. "Where did you hear that?"

"It's from the book *Huckleberry Finn.*"

"Honestly, Lisa, you amaze me sometimes. Fancy remembering that."

"Aunt Hannah remembers things like that too."

"She's an interesting person, that's for sure," Mum said. They drove in comfortable silence both with their own thoughts.

Suddenly Lisa asked, "Where are we going? This isn't the way home."

"Don't you remember?" Mum said. "You're going to Ben's this afternoon. That reminds me. You'd better leave your mouse in the car." She took one hand off the steering wheel and pointed to the box at Lisa's feet. "You don't want it running away at Ben's place."

Ben was Lisa's friend. He went to Lisa's school and was in a grade below her, but he had Asperger's too and didn't mind it when she did and said strange things.

"Awww," Lisa groaned. "I forgot. I don't want to go."

"Now Lisa, don't be difficult," Mum said.

"I've been out all morning. I want to go home," Lisa whined.

"Ben will be expecting you to come."

"He won't care. I bet Andy's there anyway." Andy was Ben's friend, but Lisa found him rather annoying.

"That's not the point," Mum said. "Sometimes you have to consider others before you think of yourself."

Lisa sniffed back tears. How could she consider others when every bit of energy she had went into trying to behave at the stupid party? All she wanted to do was curl up with a good book on her bed by herself.

"Oh stop it, Lisa," Mum snapped. "It's not as if I'm taking you to a torture chamber. You're going to Ben's and that's that." Mum stared hard at the road and drove faster.

Lisa pulled out the blue satin, rubbed her ears and whimpered all the way.

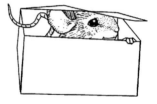

Chapter 5
The Door

When Mum pulled into Ben's driveway, Lisa slowly trudged into the house. She ignored the greetings from Ben's Stepmum, Mrs Jones, went straight to the bathroom, shut the door and changed out of the party dress into her favourite baggy shirt and shorts. At least Mum had remembered to bring those. As Lisa left the bathroom she heard her mother give an apology for Lisa's rudeness to Mrs Jones but didn't want to hear any more. If she had been allowed to go home, there would be nothing to apologize about. She found Ben and Andy playing on the computer.

"Hi, Lisa," Ben said. "Want to play?" Andy did not look up at all.

"No," Lisa said grumpily.

"OK," Ben said and turned back to the screen. Lisa moped around for a while, then wandered outside. Ben had a huge backyard, complete with a pool and a large forest area around a gully. Lisa headed down to the trees. It was cool and quiet and she wanted to be alone. The scrub was thick and overgrown and they rarely played there. Lisa crawled through the bushes, pushing the branches aside to make a tiny cubby hole up against the steep side of the gully. It was small, snug and quite dark. Mosquitoes buzzed and birds chirped and Lisa relaxed. She was alone…for now.

Squirming to get more comfortable, her arm rubbed against a rock. No wait, it was not a rock. It was a brick. A very old brick. Lisa peered around in the half-light. There was another brick and another in the ground in neat rows. She was lying on an ancient path that had been covered by rotting leaves. Suddenly a breeze blew through the bushes and Lisa shivered. But as soon as it came, it disappeared. That was strange, she thought. It's not a windy day. As she wriggled round in the narrow space, her foot hit something that made a hollow thump. Curious, she inched closer to where the sound came from. Her eyes grew wide in shock. As fast as she could, Lisa shuffled out of the scrub and ran back into the house.

"Ben," she yelled, "Come and see this."

"What?" Ben asked, concentrating on his game.

"It's amazing!" Lisa cried.

"Big deal. It's probably just a bug," Andy said. He knew how excited Lisa got over little things that didn't matter.

"Come on! I want to show you something." Without bothering to wait for them, she took off down the back garden. Ben paused the computer and he and Andy followed grudgingly. "I don't mind what it is, as long as she doesn't say a poem about it," he said.

The boys found Lisa by following her excited cries. "Come in!" she urged. Ben crawled into the tight space.

"This better be good," Andy warned as he knelt on his hands and knees.

Lisa pointed. "Look!" The two boys gasped in surprise. Set into the side of the gully and hidden behind the bushes was a solid wooden door!

"It's a secret entrance, Ben, in your own back-yard!" Lisa said. "Aren't you glad I found it?"

Ben nodded and flapped his hands furiously, unable to keep his excited body still.

"Cool," Andy breathed, no longer annoyed. "But what's it an entrance to? I mean, can we open it?"

"Let's find out," said Ben.

The three of them tore at the bushes, ripping away years of wild growth. Some of the branches were thick and hard to break.

"I'll get an axe," Ben said, running back up the slope. He returned quickly with the heavy tool in his hands. His dad was the local handyman and owned heaps of tools and he'd taught Ben how to use them safely years ago.

"Stand back," Ben called and swung the blade at the branches. One by one, the branches were broken away.

"It's an old building," Lisa said at last. "Look, it even has windows. They're boarded over."

"It must have been built right into the side of the gully," Ben said, tossing the axe to one side and flapping his hands. Then with eyes shining with excitement, he turned the doorknob. The door was stuck fast.

"It's locked," he said in disappointment.

"I don't think so," said Lisa, "There's no keyhole."

"Let me try. I'm bigger than you." Andy grabbed the knob and pulled with all his might...and the door creaked open.

Two well-worn stone steps led the way up into darkness.

Chapter 6
A Hidden Hideaway

A musty smell wafted out of the gloom.

"Unreal!" Andy said. "A hidden hideaway."

Lisa swept aside a massive spider's web and peered into the darkness. "What is this place, Ben? Why is it here?"

"I don't know," Ben said. "But our house is about a hundred years old. Dad said it was the original homestead for this area. This is probably an old shed or something from long ago."

"Does it go all the way to the house?" Andy asked.

"Who knows?" said Lisa. "Maybe it does."

Ben's excitement grew. "Just imagine. There might be a secret tunnel into my house. Maybe smugglers lived here and this is how they snuck out at night without being seen. They've probably left buried treasure!"

"Or maybe this was a mad scientist's laboratory where he did horrible experiments on rats and humans," said Andy.

"Yeah! Swapped their brains!" cried Ben.

"Gross," Lisa said. "It's much more likely to be where girlfriends and boyfriends met in secret. Romeo and Juliet all over again."

"Now *that's* gross," Andy groaned.

"Let's find out," Lisa said as she ventured onto the first step.

Ben pushed in beside her. "I'm coming too," he said.

"Wait for me," Andy cried, but all three stopped still as they faced the pitch-black darkness.

"Need torches," Ben said.

"Yeah," Andy agreed, reluctant to leave their amazing find.

"You go get some," Lisa said. "I'll stay here."

The two boys ran for the house. Lisa went up one more step, trying to force her eyes to adjust to the dark. Suddenly she froze. Was that movement? Was something in there? Lisa backed down quickly, her heart beating fast. But nothing followed her. "Must have imagined it," she whispered to herself.

Just then a soft moaning sound drifted down the stairs. It wasn't loud, but it was a tone that grated on Lisa's nerves and goose bumps rose along her arms. She grabbed for her satin, hunched her head low and rubbed her ears furiously.

The boys found her moments later.

"What are you doing?" Andy said in a voice that made it clear he thought she was weird. But Lisa hadn't heard them.

"Lisa doesn't like noises," Ben explained. Unlike Andy, Ben thought it was perfectly normal that someone would rub their ears to keep out sounds they disliked. He touched her gently on the shoulder to let her know they were there.

Andy was confused. "But there aren't any noises."

"There were," Lisa sniffed. "A funny sound came from in there." She pointed into the doorway.

"Ooooooh," Andy said mysteriously, waggling his fingers in the air. "A ghooooost."

"Stop it, Andy. I did hear something."

"It's gone now," Ben said as he handed Lisa a torch. "Let's explore."

Chapter 7

Secret Rooms

Holding the powerful torches, Ben, Andy and Lisa took their first steps into the unknown. The light cast weird shadows on the rough red-brick walls and the room smelt stale. The air was still and as their feet brushed up dust from the dirt floor it swirled around in little eddies and floated in the torchlight.

"Creepy," Lisa said staying close to Ben.

Along the walls were remnants of a past age. Pots and pans hung from large rusted hooks. Tins and cans and strange implements lay in rickety cupboards beside chipped crockery and enamel bowls. Andy bumped an ancient broom, its straw head eaten by generations of mice, and it slid down the wall and crashed onto a metal pan. The noise was deafening in the confined space. More dust swirled in the air. Lisa cringed and rubbed her ears, the torch in her hand flickering light frantically over the walls.

"Ooops," Andy said. "Sorry."

"We'd better be careful," said Ben. "The more we touch, the more dust we stir up. It's hard enough to see now as it is."

The three adventurers tiptoed deeper into the gloom.

"Look," Ben said. "There's even a fireplace. I wonder what this room was used for?"

"It was probably a laundry," Lisa guessed, as she picked up a heavy iron with a curved handle. "Imagine ironing with this."

"But it's got no electric cord," Andy pointed out. "How did it get hot?"

"You put it on the stove, silly," Lisa explained. "My Granny once told me that if you weren't careful using one of these you'd get black streaks of soot on the clothes and you'd have to wash them all over again. She detested washing days."

A huge pot sat on cold coals in the blackened fireplace.

"There's where your mad scientist made his potions," Ben joked to Andy.

"It's more like what witches used," Lisa said. She began to whisper,

"Double, double toil and trouble; Fire burn and cauldron bubble."

"What?" Ben asked.

"It's just another Lisa poem," Andy complained.

Lisa ignored him. She tucked the torch under her chin so that her face glowed strangely.

In a croaky, witch-like voice she hissed,

"In the cauldron boil and bake:
Eye of newt, and toe of frog,
Wool of bat, and tongue of dog,
Adder's fork, and blind-worm's sting,

Lizard's leg and howlet's wing,
For a charm of powerful trouble,
Like a hell-broth boil and bubble."

Andy shivered in the dark. He didn't want to admit it, but Lisa was a great actress.

"Good poem," Ben said, breaking Lisa's spell. "Did you make it up?"

Lisa shook her head, "It's Shakespeare," she said.

"Shake a spear?"

Lisa sighed. "Forget it, Ben."

"Hey!" Andy suddenly said. "There's a door here." He had wandered to the back of the room and a small door was hidden behind some planks of wood. The children cleared some space and opened the door. Behind was a tiny narrow room that had been chipped out of solid rock. Rows of shelves held the occasional rusted can and grimy bottles.

"It's cold in here," Lisa said, rubbing her arms. "It must be the cellar where they kept food from spoiling before fridges were invented."

She left the boys to search the shelves, when she discovered another room that led from the laundry off to the right. In it, a row of old cupboards filled one wall and two rickety beds were on the other side. "Someone slept here once," she said to herself in surprise, shuddering at the thought of living in such dark conditions. Then she remembered that the windows were boarded over. A sudden faint moaning sound circled the room. Lisa froze as Ben and Andy entered the sleeping quarters.

"Did you hear that?" Lisa asked.

"What?" Ben said.

"I didn't hear anything," Andy said as he opened a cupboard. Lisa relaxed a little. Perhaps she'd imagined it.

"Hey, it's still got stuff in it," Andy said in surprise. "It's as if everyone walked out years ago and left their things behind."

"I wonder why they left in such a hurry?" Lisa asked.

"The smugglers got them," Ben said in a spooky voice.

"The mad scientist turned them all to toads," said Andy.

"You boys are so childish," Lisa said.

"Huh," Andy grunted. "At least we don't keep hearing things."

"Hey kids! Come for afternoon tea!" a voice called in the distance.

"That's Dad," Ben said. "Better go."

"I don't want to eat," Lisa said. "Let's tell him about this place, and ask him if we can stay here."

"He already knows," Ben said, heading for the stairs. "I told him when I got the torches that we found a door to a secret room."

"I don't think he believed you though," Andy said.

Lisa followed the boys reluctantly. She wasn't hungry and the mysteries of the room were much more interesting than food. Once she was outside, Lisa stopped and looked back at the little hut nestled into the bushes. It seemed sad and lonely. For a moment she could have sworn she saw a face staring out of the darkness, but she blinked and it was gone.

Chapter 8
Food, Horrible Food

Mr and Mrs Jones had arranged a lovely afternoon tea on a table beside the pool. Lisa's Mum was there too, smiling as her daughter and the two boys came into view. She tried not to mind that Lisa was grubby and had cobwebs in her hair.

"Hi sweetie," Mum said. "I thought you might be tired after the party this morning and I decided to collect you early."

Lisa sighed. The last thing she wanted now was to go home. "I want to stay," she said grumpily.

Mum gave her a sideways look and wrinkled her forehead. Lisa didn't usually understand her Mum but she knew that look. It meant that Mum was not happy. Lisa sat at the table and glared sourly at the food. There wasn't one thing she wanted to eat. Ben and Andy happily took huge helpings of cake.

"You're not eating anything, Lisa?" asked Mrs Jones.

"No," Lisa said crankily. Why do grown-ups say things that are obvious? She had no food in her mouth, therefore she wasn't eating. So why bother to comment. People were very irritating sometimes. She'd rather be alone. "Can I go back to the laundry?" she asked.

Mrs Jones looked puzzled. "Why do you want to go to the laundry?"

"The one I found in the gully with all the old stuff."

Mrs Jones was still puzzled. She looked at Lisa, then Andy, then Ben, hoping that somehow she would understand.

"I told Dad," Ben explained. "We found a secret room. It must have been an old laundry and there's a cellar and a bedroom too."

Ben's parents stared at each in amazement. "I thought you were playing a game," Mr Jones said at last. "Do you mean to tell me that you kids have discovered an old room down in the gully?"

"Three rooms, not one," Ben said, wondering why his parents were so slow. "I just told you that."

"Show us," Mr Jones said, intrigued and getting to his feet.

Lisa was up first and took off for the gully. Ben and Andy each grabbed an extra piece of cake and followed close behind with the adults trailing more slowly.

The grand tour did not take long. Mrs Jones was thrilled. "It's amazing. Imagine this being here all this time and we didn't even know it existed."

Lisa's Mum was not so happy. With Lisa's torch, she shone the light at the gaps in the slatted ceiling above her head. "Do you think it's safe for the children to play in?"

"Should be," said Mr Jones as he moved his torchlight all over the ceiling and walls. He was a handyman and knew lots about buildings and safety. "They built things to last in the olden days, and this place appears pretty sturdy to me. I suppose the roof is the biggest worry. It's been covered by dirt for goodness knows how long, but the beams are still solid. It's possible we could even use these rooms ourselves some day. Of course snakes and spiders are another matter. As long as the kids are careful, I think they should be all right."

"It's certainly an amazing find," Lisa's Mum said. "But Lisa, we have to go. We have to collect your father from work and we're already late."

"Can I stay here a bit longer?" Lisa begged.

"I'm sorry, Lisa, but we have to go." She gave *that* look again.

Lisa slumped her shoulders and trudged from the rooms.

"Say thank you to Mr and Mrs Jones," her mother called. But Lisa ignored her and stomped up to the car. She had nothing to thank them for. Life was so unfair.

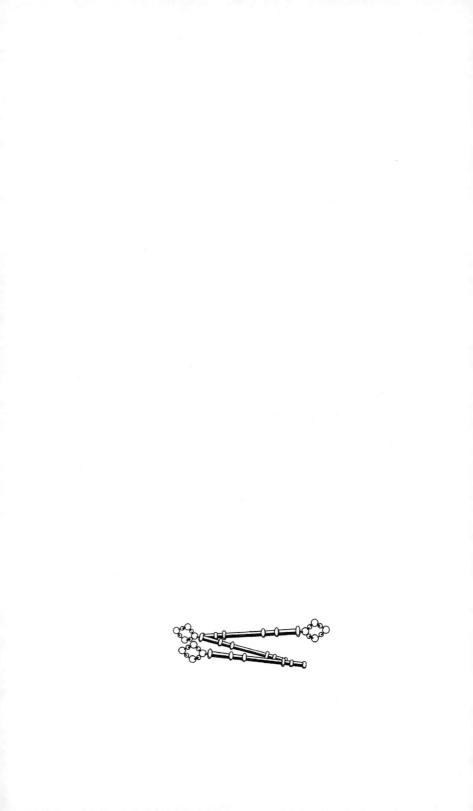

Chapter 9
Night Lessons

Lisa was in a dreadful mood all evening. She refused to have dinner and only ate a tiny bit of apple for dessert. As usual, it had to be sliced to just the right thickness.

"What's the matter, Lisa?" Dad said as he later sat by her bed. "You haven't exactly been pleasant company tonight."

Lisa sniffed back tears. "I had a terrible day."

"That's not what I heard," Dad said. "Mum told me how well you got on with Aunt Hannah and then how you discovered a secret room at Ben's house. That appears to be an amazingly good day to me."

"Mum made me go all that way to the stupid party and she knows I hate meeting people, and then she wouldn't let me stay at Ben's. It's not fair."

Dad was quiet for a moment and then turned to Lisa. "So you believe that Mum has been mean to you today and that makes you angry?"

"Yes."

"Ahh," Dad sighed. "And have you thought about how Mum feels about all this?"

"No. Why should I?"

"Do you know why your mother took you to the party?"

Lisa shook her head.

"Mum knows that Asperger kids find it hard to meet people. You like to be by yourself. She was hoping that being with family, and having her by your side, would make it easier for you. It's important that you learn how to be polite and how to mix with others. You will be meeting new people for the rest of your life, Lisa. What you learn now will help you later on when we can't be with you. And," Dad added, "her idea worked. You met Aunt Hannah and had a good time."

Lisa shrugged. That made sense. Sort of.

"And then even though she knew you were tired, she made you go to Ben's. Not to be mean to you, but because it's important to keep your promises and you told Ben you would be coming."

"Ben wouldn't have cared if I didn't come," Lisa said sullenly.

"No, he mightn't, but then again he might. How can you be sure? You can't change your mind simply because you don't feel like doing something, especially with your friends."

"It's hard." Lisa wanted to cry again. Her Dad gave her a hug. His strong arms felt good around her and she let him hold her for a little longer than usual before pulling away.

"Think of the good times you had today, Lisa. Don't dwell on the bad. And," Dad said as he got up and turned off the light, "you'd better apologize to your mother."

Lisa lay in bed and thought about her day. She remembered the long chat she had with Aunt Hannah. What a lovely lady she was. And then she recalled the excitement of finding the secret room and the mystery of the noises and the strange face she thought she had seen. It *had* been an amazing day. Dad was right.

Suddenly Lisa felt hungry. She got up and headed for the kitchen, but then turned and went to her mother's room instead. She had an apology to make first.

Chapter 10
Metal Detecting

Next morning, Lisa asked if she could go back to Ben's.

"If *you* ring him, but remember, we're going to see Aunt Hannah this afternoon and I don't want any tantrums when I come to collect you," Mum said.

Lisa sighed. She loathed using the phone. There was something *wrong* about talking into a piece of plastic, but Mum insisted that she use it as much as possible. "Phones are part of life, Lisa. Get used to them," she always said. Honestly, Lisa thought, these constant life lessons are tiresome.

But Lisa did ring and Ben's Mum answered the phone. Ben didn't like phones either, but was happy to talk to Lisa. "Come over straight away," Ben said in excitement. "Andy bought his metal detector and we're going treasure hunting!"

Lisa finally arrived at the old laundry. Mr Jones had obviously been busy. Thick electric cables trailed down the gully and up the steps and two large spotlights lit up the rooms. Ben and Andy were already there.

"Hey, Lisa!" Ben called. "Look what we've got." He held up the metal detector.

"I found an old coin." Andy showed her a battered penny.

"And all this stuff," Ben added, as he pointed to a pile of assorted nuts and screws and bits and pieces. Little holes littered the floor where the boys had dug up their treasures.

"Can I try?" Lisa asked.

"OK, but go into the bedroom. We haven't tried there yet."

Not quite sure what she was doing, Lisa took the machine and started scanning the floor. Almost immediately the buzzer sounded.

"Hold it," Ben cried. "I'll dig." He got on his hands and knees and stabbed the hard dirt with an old screwdriver. It hit something hard and Andy brushed away the soil with his fingers.

"Just another piece of tin," Andy sighed. "But that's life. Nothing exciting is buried in here. The only interesting thing is my coin and we've been digging for ages."

"I want to try again," Lisa said. She waved the metal detector over the floor and it buzzed straight away. Ben did not take long to dig up a small rusted buckle.

"I wonder who wore this?" Lisa said, holding it carefully. "Imagine a beautiful lady slipping on her shoes, buckling the dainty straps so she could dance all night at the ball."

"Yuck," Andy groaned. "Do you always have to do that?"

"Do what?"

"Talk about mushy stuff all the time. I mean that's just a grubby buckle. It probably came off an old boot."

"Maybe the evil scientist used it to strap his victims to a table!" Ben said grinning.

Andy smiled. "Now *that's* interesting."

"You boys are hopeless," Lisa sniffed, turning on the metal detector again. "The past is beautiful. That reminds me of…"

"Oh no!" Andy cut in, pretending to be scared. "Help, Ben! Lisa is going to say another poem. Let's get out of here while we can."

"Great," Ben said. "Want to play multi-player?" Ben's Dad had linked two computers in the house and now the boys were able to sit at their own screens to play the same game. Ben hadn't touched the computer since the room was discovered. This was the longest time for ages that he had gone without playing a computer game.

"Do you want to come with us, Lisa?" Ben asked.

"No."

"Suit yourself," Andy said, and the two boys raced outside.

Lisa briefly wondered why Andy was talking about a suit. "Honestly," she thought, "That boy is so odd." Then she breathed a sigh of relief. It was good to be alone. It meant she didn't have to consider what others wanted or how they were feeling or have to make small talk. To have this wonderland to explore all by herself was sheer pleasure.

Lisa stood in the middle of the bedroom as dust floated around her in the glare of the spotlights. Through the haze she examined the floor and walls. What a small room, she thought. Only just enough space to walk and to sleep. Then she recalled that Ben and Andy had dug up the walkways in the other rooms and had found nothing exciting. Maybe the things worth finding were hidden out of the way. Carefully Lisa pulled one bed away from the wall and slid the metal detector into the gap. It gave a strong buzz and, once she located the exact spot, she began to dig. A glint of gold shone in the dirt.

A brooch! Lisa held it to the light. It was long and thin, but heavy and had lovely engraving on the front. She turned it over and squinted to make out the writing on the back.

William Cotton

William Cotton. Could this be a boy's brooch?

Suddenly she became aware of a faint moaning from behind her. She spun around but saw nothing. It was the same sound she had heard yesterday. What was it? Could it really be a ghost? Lisa shuddered. It was such a strange unearthly sound. She grabbed her satin scarf and rubbed her ears furiously.

After some moments, she stopped rubbing and listened. No more sound. All was quiet. Wait…what was that? Through the doorway there was movement in the laundry. Ben must have come back for something. Surely he heard the noise this time. But when she peered around the doorway, the laundry was empty. Or was it? A flash of black, like the trailing hem of a long skirt, disappeared into the cellar.

"Who's there?" Lisa called nervously. No answer. The dust hung still and unmoving in the beams of the spotlights. No one has been walking through here, she thought. She tiptoed to the cellar and pushed the door fully open. It was empty. Whatever or whoever had been there had vanished.

Chapter 11

The Present

Lisa was quiet on the way to visiting Aunt Hannah that afternoon. She hadn't told anyone about what happened in the morning. If they didn't believe she had heard noises, then they'd never believe she actually saw anything. Even Lisa doubted herself. Things don't vanish. It was impossible.

When they arrived at the nursing home, Lisa had almost convinced herself that she had imagined everything.

Lisa and her mother had to walk down a long corridor to get to the room. Aunt Hannah greeted them at the door, leaning heavily on a walking frame. She wore a lavender chiffon dress with huge frills along the sleeves. "Lisa, Mandy! How lovely to see you," she said. She showed them around her tiny home. She had one room with a toilet and shower all to herself.

"Sorry about the lack of space," she said as she sat heavily onto the only lounge chair. "Mandy, you can sit on my bed and Lisa, you can sit in my wheelchair."

Lisa settled into the chair and rested her hands on the wheels. She pushed herself backwards and forwards a little. It was fun.

"This is very cosy," Mum said peering at the shelves full of oddments and photos.

Aunt Hannah smiled. "This will be my last home, so I thought I'd make the most of it while I can."

"Why don't you have a stove?" Lisa asked.

"No need. They cook for me here. There are some benefits to growing old."

Mum frowned. "I remember my mother telling me one of your past jobs was cooking."

"I cooked when I was a servant girl. Gosh, that must be sixty years ago now."

"I thought you made lace," Lisa said.

"I did that too. It was my hobby. Something I did for myself after my work was done for the day. By candlelight. No electricity back then. You have TVs and computers these days, but I had none of that. When the lady of the house found out how good I was she let me use her sewing room occasionally to make lace for her girls. Quite a privilege, it was."

"It's an art that's mostly lost now," Mum said. "Hardly anyone knows how to make lace anymore. Such a shame."

Aunt Hannah reached down beside her chair. She picked up a long wooden box and handed it to Lisa. "Open it. It's my present to you."

Full of excitement, Lisa took off the lid. "Wow," she whispered in awe when she peeked inside.

"They're lace bobbins," Aunt Hannah explained. The bobbins were laid out in the box on top of some crumpled pieces of cardboard. Each bobbin was about as long as Lisa's hand and was thin, resembling a round moulded chopstick.

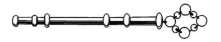

Lisa lifted them out one at a time. Some were made of rosewood, others of bone or ivory. They were decorated in different ways, two of each kind. Some were handpainted with tiny wild flowers. One pair had a weaving of pewter melded into the shaft. At the end of each bobbin was a ring of beads. Glass beads and ceramic beads. Beads with swirls and beads of gold. Tiny beads and fat beads. Together they were a treasure trove of wonderment.

"They're stunning." Lisa said. "Thank you very much."

"Which one do you like best?" Aunt Hannah asked.

Lisa touched two rosewood bobbins with silver inlay. The beads were black glass with drizzles of red and blue across them.

"Good choice. Those are very old and quite valuable. When the beads are on the end of a bobbin, they are called spangles," Aunt Hannah explained. "They help to stop the bobbins rolling around and twisting up the threads."

"Which one is *your* favourite?" Lisa asked.

Aunt Hannah gazed into the air dreamily for a moment as if remembering something from long, long ago. She pushed herself to her feet and grabbed the walking frame from beside the chair. Hobbling to a cupboard, she took a cloth pouch from a drawer, then slowly shuffled back to her seat. She fumbled inside it until she found what she was seeking. "Here, dear," she said. "This is my favourite."

Aunt Hannah held up a bobbin. It was different from the others. It was all wood and had a much fatter base. There were no decorations and no beads. "It's called a continental bobbin," she explained as she handed it to her Great Niece. Lisa rolled it between her fingers, enjoying the smooth hardness of the wood.

Outside a sudden breeze picked up and stirred the curtains in the open window. Aunt Hannah flinched. "Shut that for me, be a dear," she said nervously. "I don't like wind."

Lisa did as she was asked. "Strange," she thought, "it's not at all windy outside." She gave the bobbin to her mother as she sat back down.

"It's very plain," Mum said. "And old. And the wood is cracked. Why is it your favourite?"

"Someone very special to me made it, that's why."

"I prefer the spangled ones," Lisa said.

"Of course you do. They're much prettier."

"Aunt Hannah," Lisa said eagerly, "Would you teach me how to make lace? Please?"

The old lady smiled. "I was hoping you'd ask that."

Chapter 12

The Lacemaker

"I first learnt to make lace when I was about your age," Aunt Hannah said. "In fact I worked in a house not far from here. Mind you, it was the only house for miles. We had to go by horse and cart for hours on a dirt track to buy supplies. Strange isn't it, how time moves in circles? I was born here, I've travelled the world and now I'm back. I began as a servant, and now people wait on me."

"Which house did you live in?" Mum asked.

"The big one on the hill. It had a huge verandah all around it. We needed that for the shade. It got terribly hot in summer."

"That's Ben's house!" Lisa cried.

"You know the place?" Aunt Hannah asked.

"My friend Ben lives there! I visit all the time. We found some underground rooms. Did you live in them?" Lisa bubbled with excitement.

"Underground rooms? The servants' quarters and the laundry? Fancy them still being there," Aunt Hannah marvelled. "Yes I did live in them once, but that was a long time ago."

"*You* lived in those rooms!" Lisa cried in excitement. "Ben won't believe this!"

"They were built into the side of the slope under the kitchen," the old lady explained. "Often houses in the old days had kitchens and laundries away from the main house because of the fire risk. All the food and hot water had to be carted along walkways to the house. Such a job it was. After I left the house I heard that the owner removed the kitchen. They must have left the laundry and the quarters behind and covered them up.

"Wow," Lisa sighed, then suddenly remembered the brooch she had found. It was still in her pocket. She'd forgotten all about it until now. "Did you ever know someone called William Cotton?" she asked.

Aunt Hannah stared at Lisa in shock. "Goodness child," she said. "How do you know about him?"

"I found this brooch," she said, handing it to her aunt. "It was under one of the beds."

Aunt Hannah took it with care. "It's not a brooch," she said softly with a voice full of remembering. "It's a tiepin. And, yes. I did know William. He was the son of the owner of the property. The Cotton family was highly respectable and well known in the district."

"Why would his pin be in the servants' quarters?" Lisa asked.

"I couldn't possibly say," said Aunt Hannah stiffly. "I can tell you though, he was rather sweet on me."

"What does that mean?" Lisa imagined a man tipping sugar all over her Aunt.

"He liked me. He used to call me Hannah Honeybunny. I know it's a silly name but it was special to me."

"How romantic," Lisa sighed.

"In fact he was the person who made this," Aunt Hannah said, holding up the continental bobbin. The old lady stared at the floor as she remembered her past. "William asked me to marry him," she said sadly in a faraway voice. "He said with our names we were meant to be together. Hannah Cotton Lace sounds nice, don't you think?"

"That's lovely," said Mum. "Why didn't you marry him?"

"I was a servant girl and he was the master's son. Back then you simply didn't marry out of your station. There was so much scandal that I was sent away. Packed my bags and left. Never saw him again."

"That's sad," Mum sighed. "So that's why you never got married at all."

"Never found anyone else as nice," said Aunt Hannah.

There was silence in the room as the three thought about the past. Lisa finally said, "Did you ever...?" She paused trying to get the words right. "Did you ever hear things when you lived there? Like "woooooh" sounds?"

"Oh yes, of course," Aunt Hannah answered. "The windows were terribly ill fitting and when the wind blew, it made a howling through the cracks, that's for sure. Sounded spooky, especially when the candles were out."

Lisa nodded. That made sense, but there hadn't been any wind yesterday...had there?

"What about seeing things? Were there any ghosts? One that wore a black skirt maybe?"

"Black-skirted ghosts? What an imagination you have, Lisa," Mum said.

But Aunt Hannah's eyes grew large and she gaped at Lisa with surprise.

"The Lacemaker!" she said. Her hand shook as she placed it on Lisa's shoulder. "Goodness me, child, I haven't heard about the Lacemaker for years. That brings back memories. After I left, there were many stories in the district of the ghost of a woman in black living in the kitchen, searching for something. I thought those stories stopped when they took the kitchen away. Never believed a word of it, myself." But Aunt Hannah's old hands kept shaking.

"Who was the Lacemaker?" asked Lisa.

Aunt Hannah looked away, deep in her thoughts. Dropping her head, she said, "It's not something I want to remember, child."

Mum turned to Lisa. "Time for us to go." She didn't know what Aunt Hannah was so disturbed about, but she wasn't surprised that her aunt had secrets in her past. Aunt Hannah had always been a bit quirky. It was almost a family joke. When someone was being silly, others would say, "You're as batty as Aunt Hannah."

As they drove away, Lisa glanced back at her Great Aunt's room. The curtains rippled softly behind the closed window.

Chapter 13
School

"Lisa! Will you please pay attention!" Miss Reed, her teacher, said in frustration. "At least *try* to catch the ball. That means keeping track of the game and knowing when it's your turn."

Lisa was on the playing field with the rest of her class practising ball games. Even at the best of times Lisa was poor at sport. She never was able to catch a ball properly or kick a goal or even follow rules of a game too well, but this week it was even worse. In fact everything lately had been unbearable. Mum refused to let her go to Ben's after school until she'd done the week's homework and that took ages because Lisa saw no purpose in homework and instead did everything she could to get out of doing it.

But that did not stop her from taking the bobbins from the box that Aunt Hannah had given her, and examining them over and over again. In fact, some of the bobbins were in her pocket right now. She also had one of the crumpled pieces of cardboard. Lisa had nearly thrown the cardboard pieces away the first time she took them from the box, believing they were rubbish. But looking closer, she saw that they were covered in tiny pinpricks. When held up to the light, an elaborate pattern could be seen. Lisa found a book in the school library on lace and discovered that each of these pieces of cardboard was called a lace pricking, or a pattern. But who was the Lacemaker? Lisa couldn't keep this mystery out of her mind.

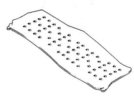

A flicker of movement from the corner of her eye made Lisa turn. She'd been seeing glimpses of…of something ever since she'd entered the secret rooms last Saturday, as if something was following her and ducked out of sight each time she glanced its way. But this time a ball hit her on her cheek and she flinched with the pain.

"Are you OK, Lisa?" Miss Reed asked, half in concern, half in exasperation. "I told you to keep an eye on the ball."

"I kept a cheek on it," Lisa said, "Isn't that good enough?"

Miss Reed grinned. Lisa was a strange kid but she had a great sense of humour. "Do you want to sit down for a while?"

Lisa nodded. Not because she was really hurt but any excuse to get out of sport was good enough. It wasn't long before the bell rang for lunch to start. Lisa wandered back to her bag to get her sandwiches, always with cheese grated exactly the right thickness, when she saw Ben in the distance.

"Ben!" she called, "Wait for me!" but he didn't hear and was soon caught up in the crowd of kids and out of sight.

"So," said a voice behind her. "It's Ben, is it?"

Lisa turned and cringed. It was Thomas, a boy in her class who constantly annoyed her. He had a few friends with him and they were all sneering nastily.

"Was that your boyfriend you were calling to?" another boy sniggered.

Lisa stared at the ground and didn't answer, hoping they'd go away. They didn't.

"Come on, answer me." Thomas poked her softly on the arm.

Lisa winced. She did not like being touched and he knew it. "Leave me alone, Thomas," she demanded.

"In a bit of a bad mood today, are you?" Thomas said, "Answer my question and I'll go. Is that kid your boyfriend?"

Lisa thought about the question. Ben was her friend and he was a boy, therefore he was her boy friend.

"Yes," she snapped and tried to walk away.

"Oooooh, lovers!" cried one boy.

"Kissy, kissy!" smirked another.

"It's not like that!" Lisa shouted. "He's just my friend. Now leave me alone!" She pulled the scarf from her pocket and began to rub her ears furiously, trying to hide the sound of his voice. Thomas grabbed her hand and pulled it away from her ears. "Weirdo!" he yelled in her face. His fingers dug in her wrist and it hurt! Scared and confused, Lisa pushed Thomas hard. Then she ran and ran and ran.

Chapter 14

The Reserve

When Lisa was younger, she had often run away from school. When kids got too loud, or her clothes were too hot and scratchy, or she was bullied, she ran. At first the running itself made her feel better. She enjoyed the rhythm of her feet thumping on the footpath and the wind in her face. As she got older she'd run to a safe place…back home or to her cubby hole or into the scrub where she hid from the world.

But this time she ran blindly with no thought in mind. By the time she slowed down, Lisa realized she was lost. Somehow she'd run to the reserve at the back of the school grounds where kids weren't allowed to go. Here, the vegetation was left as natural as possible to allow the native wildlife to live in peace. Lisa stopped and, breathing hard, wondered what to do.

And then she saw something. A flash of black darted behind a tree. Maybe it was a cat? She had heard about feral cats hunting in the reserve. Lisa crept closer, trying not to scare it away. But then, from the corner of her eye, she saw a flicker of movement deeper in the trees. No animal could move that fast. Besides, it was more like the swish of a skirt.

A long black skirt? A moment of realization struck Lisa. Could this be the Lacemaker who Aunt Hannah spoke about?

Without considering the danger she might be in, without thinking of how worried her teachers would be when she didn't turn up for class, without reasoning beyond her own curiosity, Lisa followed the black shadow deeper and deeper into the woods.

"Lisa! What are you doing here at this time of day?"

Lisa forced herself to focus on the voice. Her eyes were blurry and her brain was a fog. Where was she?

"Are you OK?"

Lisa knew that voice. She looked around in amazement. She was on Ben's property down in the gully and Mr Jones was staring at her in alarm.

"I…" Lisa stopped. What could she tell him?

"I…I got lost," she said finally. That was the truth. "A bully hurt me and I ran."

"Of course," Mr Jones said understanding at last. "The reserve runs between our land and the schoolyard. Have you run all that way through the bush? You're lucky you ended up here. You could have been miles away by now."

Lisa hung her head, but from beneath lowered eyes she peered around. Where was the Lacemaker? Once again the shadow had vanished.

"You're a lucky girl that I was here this time of day," Mr Jones said as he walked back up the slope. "I'm in the middle of a job but my mower blade broke and I had to come home to get a new one. I was in my shed when I saw you. Come up to the house and I'll ring the school."

"I don't want to go back to school," Lisa said.

Mr Jones glanced at his watch. There was only an hour to go until school finished. He sighed, "After I've rung the school, I'll ring your Mum and ask her what she wants me to do."

"She's at work," Lisa said, "Dad too. Can I go to Aunt Hannah's?"

"I'll ask your Mum," Mr Jones repeated firmly.

Chapter 15

Gwyneth

Lisa sat in Aunt Hannah's wheelchair and rolled it gently back and forward. Apart from saying hello when Lisa first arrived, Aunt Hannah had been very quiet. She wore an elaborate ivory gown with a dropped waist and a huge satin bow at the back. A long string of pearls hung around her scrawny neck. Lisa chatted on about school and why she had run away, but Aunt Hannah hardly appeared to be listening. When Lisa got to the part about following the flash of black, however, Aunt Hannah said quietly, "Her name was Gwyneth."

"Gwyneth? Who was Gwyneth?" Lisa asked.

"She was the senior maid when I was first employed at the Cotton house. She was old even then and it was my job to help her with the daily chores. We got on well and despite the age difference we became good friends." Aunt Hannah paused and twisted the pearls round and round her fingers.

"She was amazing when it came to lacemaking. She could twist a bootlace and make it beautiful. From all over the district she was simply called the Lacemaker and everyone wanted her pieces to adorn their dresses or their furniture."

Aunt Hannah fiddled with the clasp at the back of her neck and unclipped the collar of her frock. "This is her work," she said as she handed the delicate material to Lisa. "Art pieces like this were never sewn onto clothes. They always had to be removed for washing."

Lisa held the lace with care and trailed a finger over the intricate detail. "It's beautiful," she said.

"Then came Gwyneth's greatest honour," Aunt Hannah continued. "She was asked to make the lace for a christening gown for a duke's daughter in England. Her fame had spread that far! The Cotton family was terribly proud of her and William made a special set of bobbins, perfectly weighted so that her work would be faultless."

Aunt Hannah turned to her bedside cabinet and removed the cloth pouch from the drawer and handed it to Lisa.

"Was this is one of them?" Lisa asked taking out the old continental bobbin. "I thought you said it was yours."

"By then William and I were already seeing each other secretly and he promised that as soon as our friendship was public he would make me a set too."

"Did he?"

"Just listen. It is a difficult story, child. Gwyneth spent a long time on the pattern, featuring the baby's initials into the most intricate pricking I'd ever seen."

"This one?" Lisa asked, taking a crumpled piece of cardboard from the pouch.

Aunt Hannah nodded. "I was pretty good at making lace myself, after all, I had an excellent teacher, but I could never have made *that* piece of lace."

Aunt Hannah took a sip of water. "When the lace was only half made, Gwyneth discovered William giving me a kiss in my room."

Lisa scrunched up her face. The thought of kissing any boy was disgusting.

Aunt Hannah grinned. "You'll change your mind one day, missy. Anyway she was an old lady with old values and she was horrified by what she'd seen. Saw it as my fault. She told me to leave and never come back."

"That's not fair," Lisa cried.

"Maybe not, but I had to obey. I was furious and when I had my chance, I took her wonderful pattern and one of the bobbins that William had made."

Lisa gasped. That was stealing! Aunt Hannah's face filled with sadness. "I know, I know, I did wrong and I've had a lifetime to regret my actions. You see, Gwyneth died that night. She was old. Everyone mourned her and her death was not unexpected. But I always thought it was my betrayal that brought on the heart attack. The poor, poor old lady." Aunt Hannah closed her eyes, releasing a tear which rolled down her withered face.

Some time passed. Aunt Hannah rested deep in thought. Finally, and without opening her eyes, she said, "You know, child, I'm not young anymore. I won't be here for ever. Like me, that bobbin is old and cracked, and not so useful anymore. I shouldn't have taken those things in the first place and I shouldn't have them now. But there is no one to give them back to. There is no way to put things right again."

Opening her eyes, she turned to Lisa. "I want you to have them," she said. "No one I've known has ever been interested in lacemaking until now. You are meant to have them."

"What do you want me to do with them?" asked Lisa.

"I don't care. I just never, ever want to see them again, as long as I live."

Chapter 16

Lisa the Gimp

When Mum came to collect Lisa from Aunt Hannah, Lisa was well into her first lace lesson.

"See," she said happily, pointing to the pillow on her lap. "I'm making lace."

"That's all very nice, darling," said Mum, "but do you have any idea how worried about you I've been all afternoon?"

"No," Lisa said. She hadn't thought about her mother at all. Mum shook her head. It was typical of her daughter not to think beyond her own little world.

"Why did you run away from school? You know how dangerous that is. We've talked about this before."

"Thomas hurt me," Lisa said, concentrating on twisting the threads in front of her. Cross left over right. Twist right over left. Cross left over right again. The spangles chinked and clacked against each other.

"You know you have to tell the teachers if you are bullied. They will help you. You can't always run away from your problems."

Lisa ignored her mother.

"Lisa," Mum said, "Please look at me."

"I know what you look like," Lisa said, still making lace.

"Of course you do," Mum said, getting angry. "But it's polite to look at people when they're talking to you."

"Lisa," Aunt Hannah said softly, "to make lace properly, you must know where every strand lies, and what it will do next, and how the final pattern will look. You cannot simply focus on the gimp."

Lisa paused. What was Aunt Hannah saying? Mum glanced from Aunt Hannah to Lisa, trying to work out what was going on. "What's a gimp?" she asked finally.

"This is," Lisa answered, lifting a thick thread out of the finer ones. "It's there to give the lace a special texture. Aunt Hannah says I'm like a gimp."

Mum smiled, finally understanding. "Aunt Hannah is right, Lisa. You are like a gimp because you're one of a kind. But a gimp can only work if it is part of the lace. By itself it is nothing, just a piece of string. So, you have to learn to live with everyone around you, even though you might be a bit different. And that includes being polite and trying to be aware of other people's feelings."

Lisa thought a while, then shrugged. "OK," she said. "Can I go to Ben's now?"

"No," Mum said slowly, not sure if Lisa had understood anything she had said. "You haven't finished your homework. And we haven't finished talking about what happened today."

"Yes we have. I won't run away again and I'll tell the teachers if I'm bullied. If I do my homework tonight, then can I go to Ben's tomorrow?"

"I guess that's acceptable, but you still have a lot to do," Mum said carefully.

"Good. Can we go home now? Aunt Hannah said I could take this with me." She pointed to the lace pillow and her work neatly pinned into position.

"OK," Mum agreed, glad that Lisa wasn't arguing or angry. "Say thank you."

"Thank you, Aunt Hannah. It is exceedingly kind of you teach me to make lace," Lisa said politely.

Aunt Hannah smiled. "You are most welcome."

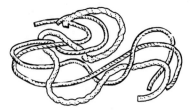

"Exceedingly kind?" Mum laughed when they got back to the car. "Where did you learn to say that?"

"It was on a TV show last night," Lisa said, worried. "Did I say something wrong?"

"No, you did well," Mum said kindly, "but at your age, a simple "thanks" would probably do."

Mum drove home with mixed emotions. Lisa could be infuriating and annoying, but at the same time was so complex and interesting. Life was certainly never boring when she was around.

Lisa also battled with her feelings. School, Thomas and his mean ways, chasing the Lacemaker through the forest, Aunt Hannah's confessions, her first lace lesson. It was all too much. More than anything Lisa wanted to curl up in bed and be alone for a while. But that luxury had to come later. As soon as she got home Lisa went to her room and opened her homework books.

Chapter 17

Over Coffee

Lisa visited Ben's house the next afternoon. But Ben wasn't home. He had drum lessons on Thursdays.

"Oh, I'm sorry," Lisa's Mum said to Mrs Jones. "I should have called before coming over. But Lisa has a very one-track mind. The only thing she's talked about this week is the old hut."

Mrs Jones smiled knowingly. "I completely understand. Ben has his special interests too. He's computer mad at the moment." She turned to Lisa, "You are very welcome to stay but you'll be on your own for about an hour."

"Great!" Lisa said. She started running to the gully.

"Lisa, say thank you to Mrs Jones!" her Mum called.

"Thank you," came a cry from the distance.

The two mothers smiled at each other. "Would you like to stay for a coffee?" Mrs Jones asked.

"That would be lovely. Thank you."

They went into the house and Mrs Jones put on the kettle. "You know, if our little Aspies ever focus their amazing concentration on something other than computer games or dusty old rooms then who knows what they could achieve!"

Lisa's Mum nodded in agreement as she helped organize a plate of afternoon tea. "Ben may well be the next computer guru. Last month I thought Lisa could become a world famous animal trainer. She's amazing with her mice. But that was last month. She has barely played with them at all this week. Now I even have to remind her to feed them. All she talks about is that old building and making lace."

"It could be worse," Mrs Jones chuckled. "Ben once had a craze on snakes!"

They sat at the table with their coffee. Lisa's Mum turned thoughtfully to Mrs. Jones. "I was wondering, does Ben find it hard to make friends?"

Mrs Jones shrugged. "He's got Andy, of course, and there are a few others at school he plays with occasionally."

"Lisa is so different from Ben. She has no friends at all. Not one. But it doesn't seem to bother her. The girls in her class are kind enough to her though. They fuss over her and make sure she's OK, but she never wants to invite them home. I worry about it more than she does."

"But Lisa's a good friend to Ben," Mrs Jones said.

"I know she calls Ben her friend, but they don't really play together. I mean, she likes him to be around, but then she'll read a book or play with her pets and Ben will go on the computer."

"I've noticed that," Mrs Jones said. "But she's a lovely girl and is always welcome here."

Lisa's Mum passed across a plate of biscuits. "What about food?" she asked. "Is Ben fussy?"

"He's got his definite likes and dislikes, but generally he eats most things."

"Yet Lisa is the fussiest child I've ever known. I worry about her diet all the time."

"Ben is quite gifted at maths. What about Lisa?" Mrs Jones asked.

"Just average, yet give her a play to learn or a book to read and she's brilliant."

Mrs Jones smiled as she poured another coffee. "There's no way you'd get Ben up in front of class reciting anything. Last time he had to give a talk in class he was so worried about it that we tape-recorded him at home and took the tape to school."

"It's strange how two Asperger kids can be so different," Lisa's Mum said.

Mrs Jones leaned across the table and added, "One thing I've learned from Ben is to try to focus on the things he does his own special way. Aspies are very interesting children and it's refreshing to see the world from a different point of view."

"Refreshing," Lisa's Mum echoed. "That's a good thought. Next time Lisa is hard to understand, I'll remind myself how boring it would be if everyone thought the same."

"Exactly!" Mrs Jones said and the two mums clinked their coffee cups in agreement.

Chapter 18

Spoon Mystery

When Lisa entered the laundry, the hairs on her arms prickled as if they'd been electrically charged. But she was too excited to be scared.

"Gwyneth!" she called. "Mrs Lacemaker! Aunt Hannah told me all about you. You can come out now. I've got something for you." She waved the cloth pouch in the air. Nothing happened. There were no ghostly noises and no apparition of a little old lady.

Lisa wandered through the rooms, back into the cellar and even checked under the beds. She found nothing, but a feeling of…of something unusual was building up inside her. Happy. Excited. Scared. Lisa stood in the middle of the laundry wondering what to do next.

Then the faint touch of a cool wind caused goose bumps to rise on her neck. A distant noise grew. A low moan, somewhere in the room. Or outside. Lisa couldn't tell where it was. She resisted covering her ears. This noise was important!

"Mrs Lacemaker!" she called.

The breeze drew Lisa to the bedroom door. Though she could feel the movement of the air, strangely the dust lay undisturbed. Lisa entered the room, feeling all at once excited and fearful, wanting to run away, but wanting to stay for an answer.

"Is this what you're looking for?" Lisa asked softly. Her eyes searched every part of the room. She walked slowly holding the pouch out in front of her.

"Aunt Hannah says sorry!" Lisa whispered.

"Hi Lisa," said a voice at the door.

Lisa spun round, dropping the pouch, her heart pounding. It was Ben!

"Did you hear a noise?" he asked.

Lisa was breathing heavily. "Now who's imagining things?" she finally managed to say.

Ben didn't notice anything unusual about Lisa. "What's this?" he asked, picking up the pouch.

"Nothing much," said Lisa, hoping he'd leave it alone.

Ben shook it open and shrugged. "It's empty anyway."

Lisa snatched it from his hands. It was true! The bobbin and pricking were gone!

Without warning, the metal detector that had been leaning against the wall began to beep. "Didn't you turn it off when you used it last?" Ben asked Lisa.

She nodded but her eyes were searching the floor. Had the bobbin and pricking fallen out? Ben checked the machine and shrugged.

"It *is* off. Must be a fault in the wiring. I'm going to dig anyway, just in case."

Lisa ignored him, and searched under the bed for the bobbin and card.

"Hey, look," Ben cried as a scrap of silver was revealed. "It's a spoon of some sort." He pulled it out and rubbed it clean.

Lisa came over and took it from him. "It's one of those special spoons you give to a baby when it's born."

Ben peered closer. "I think it says "William Cotton", and then there's a date…fourteenth of June 1913."

"That must be when he was born," Lisa said.

"Who's William Cotton?"

"It's a long story," Lisa replied. She did not understand what had happened. Did the detector become faulty at that very moment by pure coincidence, or was this spoon a gift from the Lacemaker? If it was, what could you do with a spoon? And had the Lacemaker really taken back the bobbin and card, or were they lost somewhere in the room? She stared at the floor, thinking hard. Then suddenly she had a fantastic idea.

"Is that possible?" Ben asked when she suggested it to him.

"We won't know if we don't try."

"Then let's do it!" Ben cried. "Race you to the house."

Chapter 19

Aunt Hannah's Surprise

Lisa's plan took a week to organize. With her Mum, Dad and Ben's help, all was finally arranged. Now Lisa stood outside Aunt Hannah's room, with one hand on the doorknob.

"Is everybody ready?" she whispered to the group standing in the corridor of the nursing home. When they nodded in return, she knocked, waited for the call to come in, then opened the door and slipped inside alone.

"Lisa. How lovely to see you," Aunt Hannah said happily, seated by the window in her lounge chair. A frilly blue dress matched her eyes perfectly. "I've missed you this past week."

"Hello Aunt Hannah," Lisa could not hold back her excitement. "It's all been put right!"

"What ever do you mean by that, child?"

"It's a bit hard to explain. I'll show you instead. Close your eyes. And don't peek."

Aunt Hannah obeyed curiously. She heard the door open and the shuffle of feet.

"OK," Lisa said finally. "Open your eyes."

Aunt Hannah did and gazed in confusion at the people in front of her. Lisa's Mum and Dad were there, but there was someone she did not recognize. Or did she? An old man leaning on a walking stick smiled down at her. His hair was thin and pure white and his face was crinkly and kind.

"Hello, Hannah Honeybunny," he said.

"But I still don't understand, how did you track him down?" Aunt Hannah whispered to Lisa as she watched William Cotton chatting to Lisa's parents. Never in her wildest dreams did she imagine seeing William again, after all these years. Lisa told Aunt Hannah the whole story, from beginning to end.

"After Gwyneth took back the stuff, I found an old spoon. It's as if she wanted me to find it so you two could be together again," Lisa whispered back. "Ben and I searched the internet and after a couple of emails we were able to track down Mr Cotton by using his name and birth date. My friend Ben knew how. He's a whiz at computers."

"Well, dear, you are amazing," said Aunt Hannah. "A real little detective. But the story about the ghost of the Lacemaker was only ever just a story. I never *really* believed it. Perhaps it was just luck that you found the spoon."

"Perhaps it wasn't," Lisa replied.

"What are you two girls talking about?" William asked curiously. "You're like two little mischief-makers plotting something together." Lisa and Aunt Hannah giggled guiltily.

"Did you know that William lives only an hour away?" Mum told Aunt Hannah.

"Really!"

"I did the same as you, Hannah," William explained. "I roamed the world then came back home again."

"He got married though. Do you mind?" Lisa asked.

"Lisa, don't get personal," her Dad warned.

"I don't mind her questions," Aunt Hannah said. She turned to William, "I'm just glad you had a happy life."

"His wife died years ago," Lisa informed her aunt. "Are you going to marry each other now?".

"Lisa!" Mum scolded.

"I like a girl who speaks her mind," Aunt Hannah laughed. "And to answer your question, Lisa, I think we're a bit too old for all that. Perhaps we'll just be good friends."

"Good friends is good…for a start," William agreed.

Lisa grinned, happy to see Aunt Hannah's surprise working so well. Then she turned to her aunt and said, "Oh, I almost forgot. I have a present for you."

"Goodness, I don't think I can take any more," Aunt Hannah said.

Lisa took a small crumpled packet from her pocket and handed it to her Great Aunt. Aunt Hannah opened it carefully and smiled in pleasure. "A lace bookmark!"

"It's my first piece ever. I want you to have it," Lisa said.

Aunt Hannah stroked the precious gift. "You've done a beautiful job, Lisa. The pattern is complex but all the ends are tied so nicely."

"And do you like the gimp?" Lisa asked, eagerly pointing out the thicker thread that wove its own zigzag path through the rest of the lace. "I wanted it there to remind you of me."

"The gimp is absolutely wonderful," said Aunt Hannah. And she was looking at Lisa, not at the lace.

Blue Bottle Mystery

An Asperger Adventure

Kathy Hoopman

Nothing is quite the same after Ben and his friend Andy find an old bottle in the school yard. What is the strange wisp of smoke that keeps following them around? What mysterious forces have been unleashed? Things become even more complicated when Ben is diagnosed with Asperger Syndrome.

Blue Bottle Mystery is great fun to read and will keep you guessing until the end.

'I read this book in under an hour and then immediately picked it up and read it again, much to my brother's disappointment ("It's my book!")... It was a wonderful to listen to his cries of "Oh now I understand," "I do that," "Aspergers – that's what I have." We shall have to buy another copy because both my brother and I love it too much to let the other have a read... Congratulations on a truly wonderful book.'

– Clare Truman (age 14)

Kathy Hoopmann is a primary school teacher and children's author who lives near Brisbane in Queensland, Australia. She enjoys camping, walking on the beach, and writing on the computer for hours on end. She is married with three children, two zebra finches, a cat and dozens of wild birds that feed on her back deck. Kathy has been involved with children with Asperger syndrome for many years.

ISBN 978 1 85302 978 3

Of Mice and Aliens

An Asperger Adventure

Kathy Hoopmann

When Ben and Andy discover an alien crashed landed in the backyard they are faced with a problem. They want to help Zeke repair his ship, but why does he ask for such strange things. Can they trust him?

Of Mice and Aliens is a book of mystery and fun. With Ben learning to cope with his newly diagnosed Asperger Syndrome, and Zeke trying to cope with life on Earth, things are not always as they seem.

'I would recommend this book to both parents and professionals. It is well written and sensitively portrays the difficulties faced by children and parents in living with Asperger's Syndrome. A list of support organisations and websites is given at the end of the story.'

– Rostrum

ISBN 978 1 84310 007 0

CPSIA information can be obtained at www.ICGtesting.com
Printed in the USA
LVOW07s1152200814

400074LV00001B/156/P